Forgotten Jade

Joelle Hope Warden

Forgotten Jade
Joelle Hope Warden
©WardenLegacy 2015
ISBN-13: 978-1519113948
ISBN-10: 1519113943

Acknowledgements

Hi, everyone, it's Joelle. This is my Fourth book. I am now 11-years-old. I'd like to note that this year I have tried to write my story in prose. Prose is a form of free verse poetry.
Like my other books, half of the royalty will go to Feed My Starving Children. FMSC is a non-profit organization that packs and sends to food to countries in poverty. The other half will go into my savings account, mostly for college.
The idea for this story was inspired by *Red Butterfly* **~A.L. Sonnichsen** and *Inside Out and Back Again* ~Thanhha Lai. Both are books of prose set in an Asian country.
I would like to thank Auntie Theresa, and my dad for helping me go through my book and giving me ideas and advice along the way. I also want to thank my mom for making the book cover again this year.
I hope you enjoy my new book. Some (not all) parts are inspired by my own life. Thank you for supporting me by reading this book.

Part One
Waiting

Mother
Things
My Name
Never
Mission
The Beginning
Lesson
Too Kind
Sleep
Sunday
Worship
Make Old Things New
Play
Jump Rope
Baby
English
The Ark
Think
One Thing
Suitcase
Please
Bye
Normal

Part 2
The Journey

**Forever
Mixed
Leaving
New
Hi
Happy
Plane
Long**

Part 3
A New Life

LAX
The House
Food
Fun
Sleep
Memories
Day One
Jade
Easy
School
Anything
Welcome
Stares
Friends
Like Me
Her Friend
Between
A Child
Real
Chosen
Past

Part One
Waiting

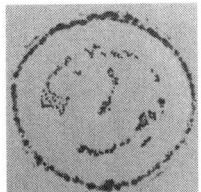

My Mother

My mother was beautiful
Her hair,
a flowing waterfall
Her lips,
a cherry blossom
Her skin,
faded paper below the
ink
But
her face
Calm ink brushes
Delicately paint the
picture
Of the one
I will never see again
The only thing she left is
One picture

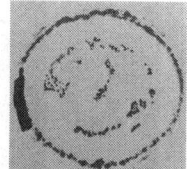

Things

I only have five outfits
One for the usual days
When we just eat, learn,
play
Bright red tops for girls,
blue for boys,
and black pants for all
One for sleep
A time where one
mustn't
make a single noise
Or
walk to the bathroom
down the stairs
Or
bother Ms. Xing
A comfy gray cotton top,
and black pants for all
One for the days
the inspector comes
To show him that we are
well cared for

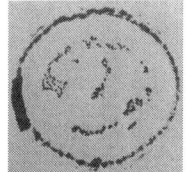

I wear a light purple
dress
It is very itchy,
but I don't have to wear
my black pants
One for Chinese New
Year
When all must celebrate
and
eat the Oranges that
bring wealth
and
sweep the old year out
the door
and
watch the dragon boats
ride down the streets
One for the day someone
will take us home
It is only to be worn on
that day
and that day only
But everyday
I will wear
My Dragon of Jade

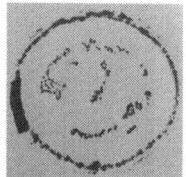

My Name

Jia Yu
Beautiful Jade
At least
that's what Ms. Xing told
me
I was put on the door
step
chewing
on a half eaten
almond cookie
Her name Jia Yu.
Please take care of my
baby.
In a package was
a picture of my mother
and
around my neck
on a gold chain was
My dragon of Jade

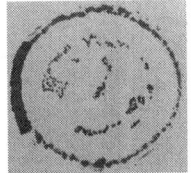

Never

"You will *never*
get adopted."
mumbles Xia Hu
"I've been here for
fourteen years."
I am eleven years old
I've lived for 11
New Year Days
I quietly sip
my chicken broth
with cabbage
and chew on my clumps
of rice

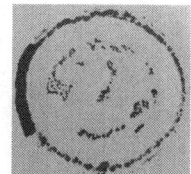

Mission

There's a knock
A knock on the door
Ms. Xing quickly
adjusts her
red business jacket
and opens the door
A man and woman
step slowly into the home
The woman has hair
the color of sand
The man has hair
the color of fire
and hair growing on his
face
They look strange
like they came
from the other
side of the world
They speak in
Cantonese
but with a
funny accent

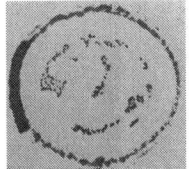

The Beginning

Ms. Xing leads us
to the front room
The lady sits down
and opens a large book
In the Beginning
God created the
Heavens
and the Earth.
She begins to read
The woman's name is
Lindsey
I hope someday
I will have a
pretty American name
just like her
The man's name is Tony

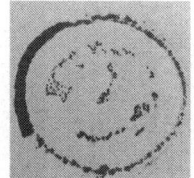

Lesson

Lindsey guides my hand
and helps me write
the characters
Heaven
and
Earth
After the lesson
The children go
to the courtyard
Meiling,
Zi Chan,
Xiu-Mei,
and I
run to the far left
to where
the purple wildflowers
grow
We make flower chains
for Lindsey
to put in her hair
Ms. Xing rings the bell
for the children
to come in

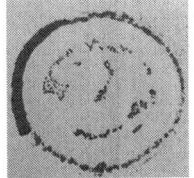

Too Kind

We run
and show Lindsey
our flowers
she smiles
and says
*You four
are too kind*
Meling asks
*Is it bad to be
too kind?*
Lindsey laughs
and tells us it means
that someone is very nice
Ms. Xing isn't always in
the best of moods but,
On her good days
Ms. Xing
teaches us fun things.
I remember
the time
when she taught us to
braid
So we
braid the flowers
into Lindsey's hair

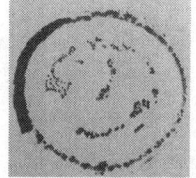

Sleep

Ms. Xing
tells us
time for bed
I wrap my blanket
around myself
like a silkworm
in its cocoon
Lindsey left me
something
on my pillow
a small panda bear
stuffed animal
So I snuggle with it
and fall asleep

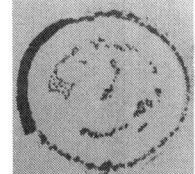

Sunday

Tony arrives at the door
with Lindsey
and two large paper bags
Lindsey helps him
put them on a table
They open the bag
I smell
salty ground pork
sweet bean paste
and savory eggs
Mrs. Ling
the cook
passes out plates
Lindsey and Tony each
take a couple boxes
and walk down
each side of the room
Steamed buns

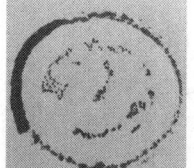

Tony sets a pork bun
on my plate
*The whole bun,
for me?*
I ask Tony
Tony smiles and says
*The whole thing.
Enjoy!*
He walks forward
to the other children
I bite into the
fluffy rice dough
It's warm
and delicious
and
I haven't even gotten to
the best part
The pork
is lightly salted
and tender.

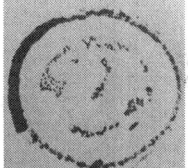

Zi Chan says
*The last time
I had a steamed bun was
the Dragon Boat
Festival!*
I nod and happily chew
This is so much better
than the Congee*
we eat everyday

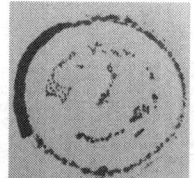

*plain rice porridge

Worship

The little children sing
Jesus loves me
this I know.
For the Bible tells me so
The older kids
like me
sit in the back
The song is
Zhiqi de*
Lindsey sings
Tony plays
his guitar
I don't sing
I'm not
a good singer

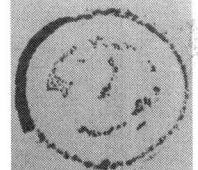

* Zhìqì de: Babyish or immature in Mandarin

Make Old Things New

It's finally over
I can finally
stop pretending
to sing
I walk to my room
for down time
and I remember my
panda
my panda Lindsey gave
me
I received my new
everyday shirt
same bright red
as always

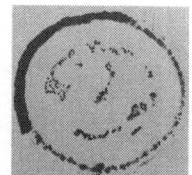

Ms. Xing
lets me borrow
her small sewing kit
because
she knows
I will take good care of it
because I have always
returned it to her
I make
the sleeves short
of my old shirt
and make
a tiny shirt
and
a tiny hat
for my
tiny panda

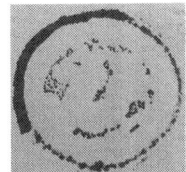

Forgotten Jade

Play

Lindsey
comes into the room
Xiu-Mei
has also made
clothes for her
tiny tiger
out of her gray shirt
We play with them
softly
because down time
is supposed to be quiet
until Lindsey tells us
it's time for lunch

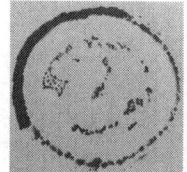

Jump Rope

Lindsey and Tony
left at lunchtime
and
came back afterwards
They brought back
a yard rope
and a ball
Lindsey teaches us how
to play
with the yard rope
I find
I am really good at it
I jump
as the rope
smacks the ground
In a steady rhythm

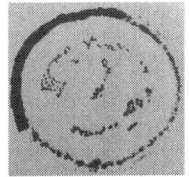

Baby

In the middle of English
class
Ms. Xing
asks me to help
with the babies
Of course I say
Yes!
When I walk
into the nursery
little Lìxúe
comes and hugs
my knees
staring at me
with a cute
little
gap-toothed grin
on her face
I pick her up
and sit her in
her high chair
as I spoon the rice
porridge
into her mouth
I remember the day
when Lìxúe arrived

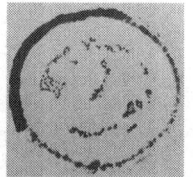

There was
a commotion
at the front door
early in the morning
4:30am exactly
a small
crying
baby
in a cardboard box
It kind of reminds me
of myself
as a baby
crying,
cold,
and alone
in the rain

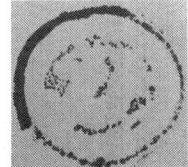

English

I continue
my English lesson
after taking care
of the babies
*I like your
dress very
much.*
Zi Chan says in English.
Thank you.
I say
You have pretty hair.
I have no idea
when I will have
to say this.
When I go to America
If I ever do
Zi Chan
seems to read my mind
groans
and nods

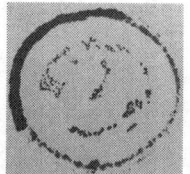

The Ark

Today
at dinner
Tony reads us
the story
about the man
with his family
with his boat
with all the animals
and how
God saved them
Amazing, isn't it?
Meiling says
I just nod
and eat my
chicken soup

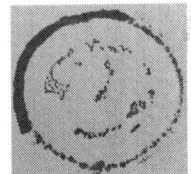

Think

I wake up
the next morning
my head hurts
so
I tell Lindsey
and she says
Rest,
I'll get Ms. Xing
and leaves
I close my eyes
Ms. Xing
gives me
a cold
face towel
We can't afford
a lot of medicine
We can't really afford
medicine at all

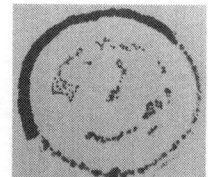

I lie down
and think
If God
created Man
and Woman
If God
saved Noah
from the flood
If God
Saved Joseph
when his brothers
sold him
If God
Gave Esther
Bravery to stand
for the Jews
If God
Sent his
One
and Only
Son
Down to Earth
To save us

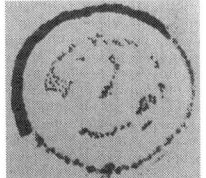

Then why doesn't he
save
me
Why did he
let my Mother
leave
me
in a
dumpster

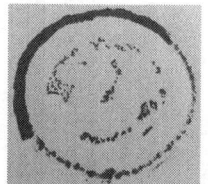

One Thing

I remember
One thing
It was
cold,
wet,
and dark
I was wrapped
in a red blanket
the note
was tucked inside
My face
was wet
It was raining
but
I think
my Mother was crying
She stood up
and ran away
in the cold
wet,
dark,
rain

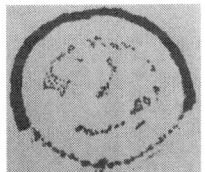

Leaving

I fell asleep
around
10:30 am
I woke
at noon
Lindsey
takes me
downstairs
I eat my lunch
and do my
brush work
I feel a hand
on my shoulder
It's Lindsey
Tony and
I are leaving
Tomorrow.

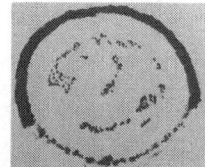

The words
are lightning
to my heart
sharp,
sudden,
and painful
They can't go
They are what
makes
everything
better
here

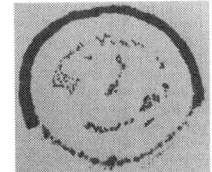

Please

I feel
like a little kid
Please don't go!
I say
Zi-Chan
joins in
You can't leave!
Lindsey looks sad
*There are
other kids
all around
the world
like you.
We have to
share our love.*
She leaves with Tony

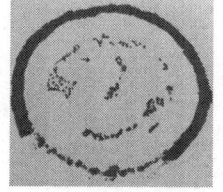

It's raining outside
so we have
extra quiet time
instead of
play time
I lie down on my
bunk
and stare at the
cracks in
the ceiling
as I feel the cracks
in my own heart

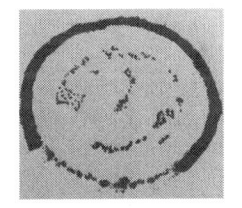

I feel the gold
chain of my
jade dragon
on my neck
I pull it up
to my face
and rub it in
my fingertips
I notice
for the
first time
it was
once broken
but the cracks
were laced
with gold
I too
am full of cracks
but yet
to be laced
with gold

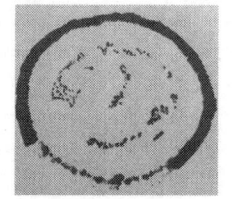

Bye

Everyone sees
Lindsey and Tony
out the door
Lindsey
is crying
I hope
you find
your forever
family
She hands me
a worn
leather bound book
read
she simply says
and
walks out the door
I think
I want to cry
but
I don't want to

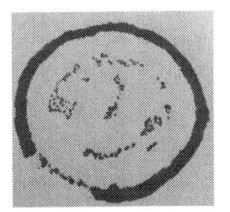

Normal

The next day
everything is normal
We eat
congee
for breakfast
We eat
rice and cabbage
for lunch
We eat
chicken soup
for dinner
We do
our lessons
inside
it's unbelievably boring
I tuck the Bible
under my pillow
and sleep

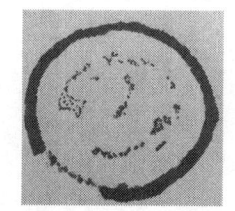

Part 2
The Journey

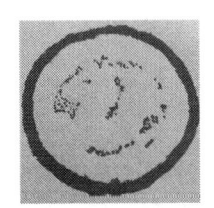

Forever

Two weeks later
I still
haven't read the Bible
Ms. Xing
comes up to me
She is too smiley
Guess what!
she says
and does
not wait
for an
answer
A family
from America
wants to
adopt you!
She hands me
a picture
of a smiling family
one girl
with
glossy black hair
One boy
with
bronze hair
and blond streaks

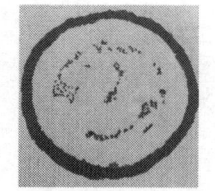

The mother
has blond hair
done up
in a fancy braid
The father
gave the boy
his bronze hair
On the back of the photo
there is
a note
Dear Jia Yu,
We are so
excited to
bring you
to California
We want you
to be happy
We want to
be your
forever family
Love,
The Carsons

Mixed

I am
excited
but afraid
what if
California
is very different
what if my English
isn't good enough
what if
they don't like me
Ms. Xing tells me
that they will come
and pick me up
in a couple weeks
I pick up my Bible
and go outside
with everyone else
for free time

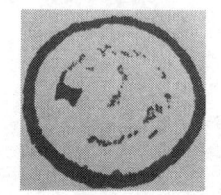

I open to a page
with a bookmark in it
Jeremiah 29:11
For I know the plans I
have for you,
declares the L ORD *,*
plans to prosper you
and not to harm you,
plans to give you hope
and a future.
Lindsey knew

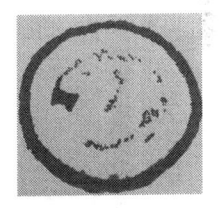

Suitcase

It seemed
like it was
only
a couple days ago
when Ms. Xing
told me
the family was coming
two weeks
all of a sudden
it became
today
I packed
my suitcase
with my old clothes
Ms. Xing
gives me
the outfit
I must wear

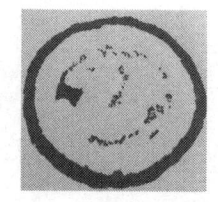

It is a
light blue shirt
with
a panda on it
and
black stretchy pants
I slip on my sneakers
and walk to the door
Meiling,
Zi-Chan,
and Xiu-Mei
run up to me
and gives me a hug
I realize
I'm crying
I've never
had a home
so why am I sad

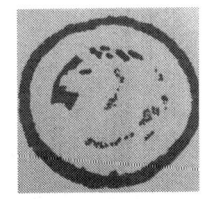

New

Ms. Xing
watches
Mr.
and Ms. Carson
like a hawk
as they
finish signing
the last
of the papers
so they can
take me to their
home

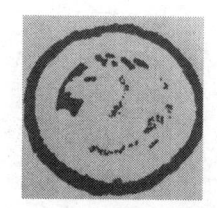

Hi

The girl
Has her hair
in a fancy looking braid
with pink streaks
she smiles
and waves
Hi,
I'm Emily
One of
the words
I remember
from
English class
Hi.
I wave
I look
at her clothes
She is wearing
a light green shirt
with a blue jacket
and gray pants
She is
so pretty
I could
never
be like her

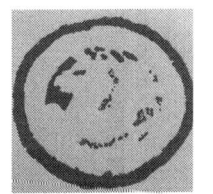

Happy

Ms. Carson
comes over to me
and squeezes me
in a big hug
Oh Jia-Yu
we are so happy
that we get
to bring you home
You're part
of our family now
Mr. and Ms. Carson,
Emily,
and
her brother Jason
lead me outside
and
we catch a
buggy
and take it
to the airport

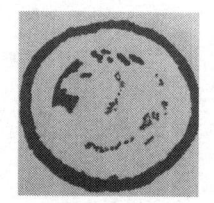

Plane

I sit down
next to Emily
*Do you want
to sit by the
window?*
I nod
and excitedly
sit and stare
out the window
Gum?
She holds out
a pink flat stick
wrapped in paper
I slowly
take it
and pull off the paper
and put
it in my
mouth
like Emily
and
chew
It's sweet,
chewy,
and juicy

Forgotten Jade

It reminds me
of this candy
Hi-Chew
that Lindsey brought
from Japan,
but this
is very
minty and sweet
like the herbal teas
Ms. Xing used to drink

Long

It takes
a really long time
to get to
California
I read the
magazine
Ms. Carson gives me
Emily
lets me listen
to her music
on her ipod
I look
out the window
when we land
so this
is California
with its
shiny lights,
big houses,
luminous cities,
and busy highways

Part 3
A New Life

LAX

*This is
LAX
says
Jason
It's where
all the planes
arrive
and take off
in LA*
It's so big
I've seen
nothing like this before
We walk
to the exit
and
we walk to a car
Hi Linda!
The woman in the car
says
This must be Jia Yu!

Then Ms. Carson says
Jia Yu,
this is your
Aunt Carrie.
I wave and
barely meet
her eye
The ride
to the Carson's house
isn't very long
When we arrive
I'm in awe
The house
It's
Amazing

The House

I dash inside
Emily helps me
carry my bags
up the stairs
there are four bedrooms
This is my room
she says
I peek in
and see
blue walls
and tye-dye bed sheets
This is Jason's room.
I look in the room
The floor is covered
with papers,
magazines,
video game cases
and so many more things
It's a mess.
Emily says
She walks down the hall

This is your room
I look inside
It's purple
Purple walls,
Purple bedspread,
a purple lamp shade,
and a lot of purple things,
but there is a green bean
bag
*I put some stuff
on the shelf for you*
Emily says
Thanks
I say
Emily asks
me if I
am okay
I nod
and she leaves me
to myself

I look on the shelf
There is some clothes
New,
cool,
and pretty
American clothes
I set them back down
I pick up the next thing
It's a small collection
of books
I have a hard time
reading the titles
Random characters
floating on the page
Like reading
a book from an outer
world,
but I remember Ms. Xing
saying,
hǎo shū rú zhì yǒu*
So I hope to learn
quickly
I put them back
I feel tired
so I curl upon the bed
and fall asleep

---

* *Hǎo shū rú zhì yǒu:* A popular Chinese phrase that means "A good book is a good friend."

Food

Emily wakes me up
Let's have dinner
I follow her
down the stairs
and to the kitchen
I sit down
In the empty seat
next to Emily
and Ms. Carson
There is chicken,
and fluffy white
stuff in a bowl
Mr. Carson says grace
and everyone starts
eating
I pick up the metal
utensil
on my right
and poke it
into the chicken pieces

I watch how Ms. Carson
eats her food
she scoops the white
stuff
onto her plate
and uses the flat
utensil to eat it
I try to copy everyone
else
It's hard at first,
but it gets easier

Fun

After dinner
Jason shows me
the video game console
we play this game called
Super Mario Bros. Wii ©
We play it on the *Wii*
It's spelled *W-I-I*
but, it sounds like
Wee
I've never played
anything
like it before
I'm pretty terrible at it
but it's fun
time passes by
quickly
and before I knew it
Ms. Carson tells
Jason and I
to go upstairs

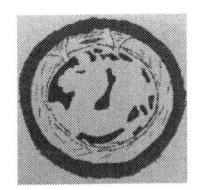

Sleep

I walk up the stairs
and into our bathroom
there is a new toothbrush
my own tube of
toothpaste
and a small towel
There are two sinks
We always used
the pump outside
in China
Emily helps me
with the sink
and I brush my teeth
I go to my room
and change
into Emily's old pajamas
I crawl
under my covers
and dig through my bag
for my panda
I find it still
with its red hat
and sweater

Ms. Carson
comes in
to check on me
Jia-Yu
are you ready
to go to bed?
I nod
Yes, Ms. Carson
She smiles
Goodnight
and shuts off the lights
I lie in bed
It's only noon in China

Memories

I look in my bag
and try to find my bible
I feel a leather spine
and pull it out
It's not my bible
It's
a photo album
I turn on
a flashlight
that was on the desk
and look at the pages
A picture of me
as a baby
in my box
A picture of me
with Zi-Chan,
Meiling,
and Xiu-Mei
in the courtyard
when we were very
young

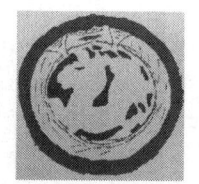

A picture of me
holding my paper lantern
on Chinese New Year
A picture of me
on my birthday
holding an almond
cookie
There are many more
almost
too many

Day One

I woke up
and walked downstairs
I found Ms. Carson
in the kitchen
Would you like
some cereal?
I remember the time
Lindsey brought
a small box of cereal
from the airport
She let me try some
and I really liked it
It was crunchy,
sweet,
and sugary
So I said
Yes please
She poured some
into a bowl
with some milk
and gave me
the bowl
and spoon

I sit down at the table
and eat my cereal
Ms. Carson comes
and sits next to me
Ms. Xing told us
a lot about you
and we have your
official American name
I told Ms. Xing
how much I'd love
an American name
What's my new name,
Ms. Carson?
I wait eagerly
on the edge of my seat
She smiles
Your name is
Jade.
And please
you can call me
Mom.
I don't want to
call her mom
at least not yet
she's not my mom

Jade

I am
Jade
I am
someone new
I am
not the same person
I used to be
I pull my dragon
off my neck
I rub it in between
my fingers
the bottom pops open
a piece of paper is inside
I read it
Wherever you go
go
with all of your heart.
-Confucius
I need to be
in this family
with
all
of my
heart

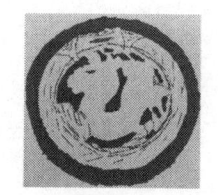

Easy

Ms. Carson
went to work
in the afternoon
so Jason
and Emily
take me to the park
Jason
sees some boys
playing
at the basketball hoop
He says something
to Emily
and jogs off
to join them
Is it that easy
to make friends
Easy enough to have
so many

School

*Are you
ready for school?*
Emily says
I've never
been to school
I've had lessons
at the children's home
but I've never
been to school
I shrug
and look at the ground
Emily is quiet
then she says
*You've never been
have you?*

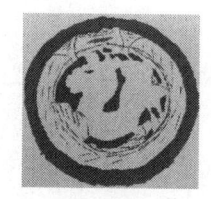

Anything

the next day
Ms. Carson
takes us all
school supply
shopping
I stand
in front of a wall of bags
to carry my books
I look at Ms. Carson
Which one can I get?
She smiles again
Any one,
Any one you want.
Those words
ring in my ears
for I
never
got anything
or everything
I wanted

Welcome

After a few days
It's the first day
of school
Ms. Carson
drops us off
at the front door
Emily shows me
where my classroom
is and hurries off
I sit down at a
desk that has
a name tag on it
that says *Jade Carson*
I look around
There's a girl
with fair skin
light hair
like Lindsey's
but has green eyes

She whispers
to a girl next to her
with tan skin and
round dark eyes
both with glancing looks
my way
A woman with
dark blue eyes
and orange hair
with a few freckles
walks to the front of the
classroom
She wears a
white suit jacket
and a black skirt
Hello class
My name is
Mrs. Davis
Lets go around
the classroom
and share a little bit
about yourself

The girl with the
green eyes starts
Hi everyone
my name is Tiffany
I do Gymnastics
and volleyball.
I have two sisters.
and have a Cat named
Meredith.
I named her after
Taylor Swift's cat.
My favorite color is
purple.
I listen as everyone else
talks
but when they come to
me
there are no words
in my mouth

Stares

I'm silent
Everyone stares
Words race in my mind
The only words
that come out are
I am Jade
Everyone stares
they wait
and wait
and wait
Can you tell us more?
Mrs. Davis asks
I like red.
I stay quiet after that
Mrs. Davis
waits
Okay then
who's next?

Friends

*Nǐ hǎo, péngyǒu**
a voice of a girl
comes from behind me
at lunch
Nǐ hǎo
I say
I turn around
The girl has the same
glossy black hair
like Emily
and fair skin
Sorry, um...
Want to come
and have lunch
with our cultural group?
I'm sitting by myself
so, why not
Sure
I say
and shrug my shoulders

Nǐ hǎo, péngyǒu: *Nǐ hǎo* in Chinese means "Hello" or "Hi"
péngyǒu means friend.

I pick up
my lunch bag
that came
with my backpack
and follow her
I try to remember
the way back
Xiàng yòu*,
Wǎng zuǒbiān*,
Xiàng yòu,
Wǎng zuǒbiān

Wǎng zuǒbiān: To the left.
Xiàng yòu: To the right.

Forgotten Jade

Like Me

I walk
into the room
I look at a colorful
handmade sign
on the board
Huānyíng
Yōkoso
Maligayang Pagdating
Yindī t̂xnrạb
Chào mừng
Hwan-yeong
Boys and girls
sit at a
couple tables
The same dark hair
The almond shaped eyes
Some have tan skin
Some have creamy light
skin

Huānyíng: Welcome in Mandarin
Yōkoso: Welcome in Japanese
Maligayang pagdating: Welcome in Filipino
Yindī t̂xnrạb: Welcome in Thai
Chào mừng: Welcome in Vietnamese
Hwan-yeong: Welcome in Korean
Chào mừng: Welcome in Vietnamese

Forgotten Jade

A teacher
stands in the
front of the room
Grace,
I'm glad you brought
a new friend
to join us today.
The girl who
brought me here
Puts down her lunch box.
Sure
she doesn't look
terribly amused
I quietly sit down
Everyone looks at me
they all look like me
in a way
but I know
they are not like me
at all

Her friend

When school is over
I run out the doors
and sit on the bench
outside
and wait for Jason
and Emily
Jason jogs up to me.
Hey Jade
Emilys talking to
Heather
she'll be here in a minute
I wish that I
had someone
to talk to
I see Emily and the girl
named Heather
So I'll see you at
volleyball practice
tonight?
Emily asks

Yep,
I love
the pink chalk
in your hair.
Heather smiles
Maybe you can come
after practice and
we can do your hair
Emily and her friend
giggle and part ways

Between

Jeez, Emily
how long
did you have
to talk to Heather
Jason sighs
It wasn't that long
Emily looks a little
annoyed
Whatever,
Mom's waiting
We begin
to walk down
the sidewalk
Jason on my right
Emily on my left
The walk is silent
Jason glares
at Emily
Emily glares
at Jason
and I
stand in between

A Child

I work
on my homework
with help from Emily
Most of the work
is pretty easy
Ms. Carson walks
into the room
Emily,
Heather's here,
are you ready to go?
Emily looks up
Sure, Mom.
She dashes off
to the front door to
greet her friend

Ms. Carson bends down
Jade, I'll be back
I just need to drop
Emily and Heather
at volleyball practice.
I nod silently and
watch her rush the two
girls
out the door
I finish my homework
and walk to the kitchen
for a glass of water.
Ms. Carson left a bible
open
on the counter
I peek over at
a highlighted section

*"For all who are
led by the Spirit of God
are children of God.
So you have not
received a spirit
that makes you fearful
slaves.
Instead,
you received God's
Spirit
when he adopted you
as his own children.
Now we call him,
"Abba, Father."
For his Spirit joins with
our spirit
to affirm that we are
God's children.
And since we are his
children,
we are his heirs.
In fact,
together with Christ
we are heirs of God's
glory.
But if we are to share his
glory,
we must also share
his suffering."*

I stood there
and just stared
at those words
*"when he adopted you
as his own children.
Now we call him,
Abba, Father."*
A tear rolled
slowly down my cheek

Real

The last few weeks
things have been real
people have made fun of me
when I
eat with my chopsticks at
lunch
when I
get an A on my math test
or,
because I have slimmer eyes
or,
because I have thick dark
hair
or,
because I'm pale paper
skinned like my mother
so I cry
everyday I run home from
school
and close the door
in my room
and cry

Forgotten Jade

In art class today
we made picture frames
from old china plates and
tiles
Our art teacher called it
Mosaics
So I ran home
and went to my room
and grab the picture of
my mother
I chose the milky green
glass
and mirror shards
I slip the picture in
between
the two pieces of glass
and watch teardrops
slowly slide down the
frame

Chosen

At one time
deserted
abandoned
Others picked before me
Always an orphan
Then came the day
Chosen
I didn't fit in at first
Looked different
Acted different
But now I am wanted
And loved
My family
My home
My friends
Chosen

Past

The past
is in the past
It shaped me
But it does not
determine me
I am in
eighth grade
I play violin,
I'm part of the school art
club,
I play volleyball
I have a group of friends
who I
always hang out with
I have defined myself
I have found out who I
am
Lastly,
I come to
trust God
realizing
I belong to Him

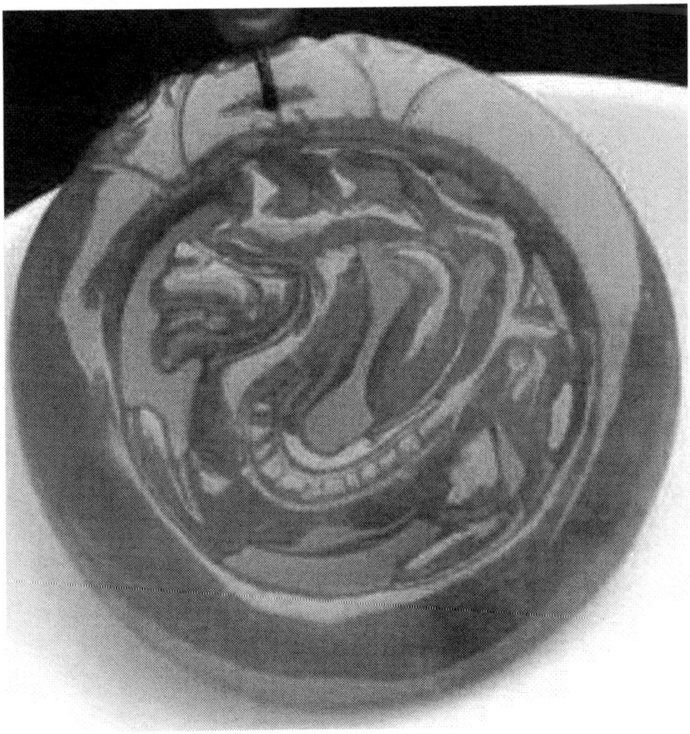

Jade's Glossary

Chào mừng: Welcome in Vietnamese
Congee: Congee is a plain rice porridge that is a popular dish in many Asian countries. It is one of the dishes served in Chinese orphanages
Hǎo shū rú zhì yǒu: A popular Chinese phrase that means "A good book is a good friend."
Huānyíng: Welcome in Mandarin
Hwan-yeong: Welcome in Korean
Maligayang pagdating: Welcome in Filipino
Nǐ hǎo, péngyǒu: Nǐ hǎo in Chinese means "Hello" or "Hi"
péngyǒu means friend.
Wǎng zuǒbiān: To the left.
Xiàng yòu: To the right.
Yindī t̂xnrạb: Welcome in Thai
Yōkoso: Welcome in Japanese
Zhìqì de: Babyish or immature in Mandarin

Forgotten Jade is Joelle's fourth book. She wrote this at the age of eleven.

You can find the rest of her writings on Amazon.

An Island and a Chance was written at the age of eight.

Letters From Brooklyn was written at the age of nine.

Silent Music was written at the age of ten.